# NIGHTFALL

# Also by Jalen Tellis

Samurai Reborn: The Black Samurai

Reckoning: A Novella

# NIGHTFALL
## STORIES

Jalen Tellis

**NIGHTFALL: STORIES**
Copyright © 2024 by Jalen Tellis
All rights reserved.
All rights reserved and printed in the United States of America. No part of this book may be used or reproduced in any manner whatsoever without written permission except for brief quotations embodied in critical articles or reviews. This book is a work of fiction. Any
names, characters, companies, organizations, places, events, locales, and incidents are either used in a fictitious manner or are fictional. Any resemblance to actual persons, living or dead, companies or organizations, or events is coincidental.

## Introduction

From the author Jalen Tellis comes a unique collection of three short stories, some of which have never been published and some that have.

"When the night falls, the fear comes to the light." In the afterword to his brand new first collection of three stories, Jalen Tellis dives into the lives of individuals who must deal with fear and ask themselves, "What's true and not true?" We live in a world of secrets, and everyone walks on it in complete fear. Tellis comes up with his stories about grief, tragedy, fear, living in our nightmares, and making us question life.

" Dream Nightmare" explores a woman who keeps having these strange nightmares. The worst part of it, the nightmare came true. In " The Girl Next Door," As a young man finally moves into his brand-new house, he encounters his neighbor Jessica Lewis, who, at first sight, falls in love with him. Jessica finally reveals her love for him on their night together for dinner. The young man rejects her, and Jessica takes the rejection...not too great. In " They're Listening," a girl tells how she witnessed her best friend encounter one of the most famous and questionable theories of all mankind.

Tellis's ability to tell these stories is something else. He will make us feel all types of emotions at once. His ideas, mind, and vision tell each of these stories. Tellis will never write something if it isn't meaningful.

For the horror fans

When the night falls, the fear comes to the light

# NIGHTFALL

# 1

## DREAM NIGHTMARE

Fall, days after Halloween, while the typical Friday night was still gloomy. I'm driving home, staring at the quiet neighborhood, just about close to my destination. I arrived home, parking in the driveway. I sit there in distress, exhausted. I rubbed my eyes as I began to breathe heavily. Luke should be asleep by now. It was 11 pm, and I told him he should be in bed no later than 10:30. I shouldn't let him stay home alone since he's only twelve. But I can't afford a babysitter. It was hard this time of year, especially as a single mother. I trust him wholeheartedly, and he hasn't given me any reason to worry for the past week.

I enter the home, turning on one of the living room lights. My home wasn't perfect. It was only a one-story home with only two bedrooms and one bathroom. The living room was tiny, with the kitchen also connecting across from each other. I placed all my belongings on the dining table and checked if Luke was asleep. I slowly open the door; he is fast asleep like a baby. I sigh in relief and am thankful he went to bed on time. I thought to myself, I still have some time to spare since I don't work until 2 pm tomorrow. I wanted to go ahead and watch a little movie. After all, I never get time for myself because I work a lot and care for Luke. I sit on the couch, grab the remote near me—and pop out the old Netflix. I didn't know what movie to watch; I just played a random film that caught my interest. I didn't remember what movie it was. But I knew it was a horror flick. Was it interesting? Yes, did I enjoy it? I don't know, because 30 minutes into it, I fell asleep.

My sleep was cut short as I woke up suddenly. I checked my phone, seeing it was midnight. It was late, and I needed to get up for work tomorrow. I guess an excellent me time isn't cut for someone like myself. I turned off the TV and started getting ready for bed.

My sleep schedule hadn't been the best, but thankfully, for my shift being at 2 pm, I can kind of sleep in. I got on my bed, put the covers on me, and began to prepare for my beauty sleep. It didn't take long for me to fall asleep as I closed my eyes, and within not even close to five minutes, I was gone.

Dreams are such a fascinating thing to have. Well, most people would agree. Sometimes dreams can come true, almost like it could be like predicting the future—but in a strangely different way. But what about nightmares? Do they predict the future? Can you have premonitions with them? I ask these questions a lot—I don't have the answers. But in this particular dream or nightmare—I finally have it.

—

I woke up suddenly in my room and looked at the clock. It was 1 a.m. In the morning. I was so exhausted and annoyed about how I woke up so late. I tried to fall back asleep, but for some reason—I can't. I kept trying, and trying, and trying. Eventually, it started to become a burden. Minutes later, I heard knocking at my room door. It was a slow and gentle knock. I didn't know who it was or who it might be as I saw a shadow of feet under the bottom of the door. Before I could even say anything, it opened drastically. It was such a slow open, making a loud, eerie creek noise. The door was now wide open, revealing a slight silhouette of someone. The figure walked forward, showing themselves. It was Luke, wearing his bright red pajamas. His eyes were different. It looked like he had bags in his eyes. It was grey and so noticeable. He looked scared and worried, and this wasn't like him. He stared at me viciously but with no emotion.

" What's wrong, honey?" I said to him, in concern.

" There's someone in my closet," He said. He left the room without me responding—walking away slowly as if I wasn't there. I had a bad feeling, a strange feeling. I got up from my bed, following where Luke was going. I go out into the hallway. It's nothing but pitch black. The only light showing is Luke's room, with the bright moonlight shining through. Luke is in the middle of the hallway, just standing. He points to his room, not saying anything. I walk into his room, nervous and scared about what will happen next. Luke's room was like any ordinary children's room, with toys and video games on the top of his dresser—posters of video game characters. I was in the center, staring at the closet. I turned to Luke, but he was already behind me. " It's something in my closet, Mommy. Can you make it go away?" He said. I looked at him in complete fear, my entire body shaking so hard you would think it was freezing in there. I shouldn't be scared of my son, but he was freaking me the fuck out. I trembled my response at him, stuttering, " I will, honey.." I slowly approached the closet door, raising my hand as it shook dramatically. I tightened my teeth and took a big gulp in nervousness. I had my hand on the handle, and without hesitation, I opened the door. It was nothing, nothing at all. Just... pitched black. I sighed in relief, turned around, and told him there was nobody. A loud and frightening scream occurred behind me as something or someone suddenly grabbed me. Holding me tight and quickly pulled me into the closet, everything darkened.

—

Then, I woke up startled. It was just a fucking nightmare. I was breathing so heavily that I was sweating. I took a few minutes to pull myself together, and finally, I started to control my breathing. I looked at my clock, and it was 1 am. Out of nowhere, I heard knocking at the door. The knock shook me, as it was slow and gentle—just like in my nightmare. The door opened; it was Luke, wearing bright red pajamas. He looked concerned and scared, just like in my dream. " Are you okay, Mommy? You look scared." He said to me. I wasn't afraid, but I was confused about seeing the parallels from now to my nightmare.

" I'm fine, honey; what's wrong?"

" I think there's something in my closet. I heard a growl, and it was calling my name." I immediately put all of the pieces together. Everything happening right now happened the same way in my dream. I quickly got up from my bed, grabbed my gun from my drawer, and told Luke to stay in my room and not come out until I said so.

I went to his room aggressively. I pointed the gun at the closet. " Who are you?" I screamed. Nothing was said; it was all quiet. Even though the silence, I still raised my gun at it, not moving a muscle.

Both doors suddenly opened rapidly. A creature, a figure, a monster screamed and rushed toward and tackled me, causing me to drop my gun. I got a look at it; it was a skinny creature. Long arms, sharp razor-sharp teeth, not even hairy, just all skin. It put its hands around my neck and began to strangle me. I couldn't move or do anything, and the monster was choking me very tightly and screaming in my face, growling. Their saliva comes out from its mouth and falls on my face. I couldn't breathe and began to feel light-headed. A gun was shot, and it felt like everything had stopped at that moment. The creature that was on top of me fell over. I was confused about what had just happened, but when I looked to my right, I saw my son holding the gun that I dropped. He dropped the gun, got on his knees, and started crying. I got up and ran to him and kept him in my arms.

As I looked at the dead creature. Its body began to break and disappear like dust, disappearing into thin air. I had no type of emotion to describe what had just happened. I didn't know what happened. I stood on the floor with Luke, trying to process everything. That dream, did I see the future? Was something trying to tell me something? I didn't know what the hell was going on. The most important question was, what was that creature, and why was it trying to come after me and Luke...

# 2
## THE GIRL NEXT DOOR

Jessica Lewis is an ordinary name to most, yet when I hear it to this day, I feel every fiber of my being shudder. Jessica was a girl who lived next door to me when I initially moved into my new home. That should have been a red flag from the beginning. But I was new to the neighborhood, and when the first pretty girl greeted me on my move-in day, how could I have seen anything wrong with that? My new place was ideal. The house's exterior was just right for me—not too enormous or diminutive—nice modern with brown color, one story with the front porch in front. But Jessica Lewis had a house more significant than any other in the neighborhood. Her house was at least three stories, with a dark blue color on the exterior walls. It looked like a mansion, too big for its size, almost like it shouldn't even belong near this neighborhood. That's how much her house stood out from the others. My house looked like an ant compared to hers.

Jessica approached me to introduce herself on the first day I moved in. She had a bright and welcoming smile, her pearly white teeth almost shining with vigor. " Hi, I'm Jessica Lewis, your neighbor," her slender arm reached out for mine, and she turned her head to the house next to mine. " I'm Darius Green, but you can just call me Dar. Nice to meet you, Jessica."

" Darius. Fancy name," she half smiled and slightly squinted her eyes. " What brings you to this quaint little neighborhood?" she asked me.

We let go of the handshake, and her fingers brushed off mine and lingered long enough for me to notice. " It was time to leave my parents. This neighborhood seems like a good fit for me," she said. Her phone suddenly buzzed, and her smile changed to a frown. " I'm sorry, I must attend to this, but I'd like to introduce myself to you properly. How does my cooking sound to you?" She asked as her eyes batted and her bright self returned.

" Oh, right now? I have to finish unpacking,"

" No, silly, dinner tonight." She giggled, and both her hands held onto her phone.

" Oh, yeah, that sounds great," I smiled.

" Okay, I'll leave you to it; see you tonight..." She pursed her lips and started walking backward. I was looking forward to coming to dinner because, once again, she had a lot of energy. At that point, I still didn't see anything wrong with her.

—

Later that night, I left the house, and my father's leather jacket fitted me more than ever. I made my way to her house—lights being strangely on, even the one upstairs. A slender woman's silhouette appeared on the window's left side. It was Jessica, but I don't know why. It was like she was watching me. The silhouette was gone, but I wasn't quite fazed by it as I was already at the front door, fixing myself up. The door opened, and gracefully, she stood in a yellow dress with sunflowers, its straps refining her toned shoulders. " Dar! I'm so happy you came," Said Jessica, her voice filling my ears, fully rounded but inviting.

" Well, I was promised food, so here I am," I said.

" Then you came to the right place," Silence surrounded us, and we were left staring at each other. There was something about Jessica, something that made my stomach churn. " What are you still doing out there? Come on in," She walks back, making a way for me to walk in. I come inside as she closes the door behind me. My eyes gazed upon the paintings and sculptures scattered around her home. My hands were starting to be clammy; my cheeks turned numb from smiling too long. The interior was incredibly wooden as if you were entering an ancient classic mansion. "This place feels very authentic," I told her.

" I'm delighted you like it. I had professionals come in and help me renovate the place." I could tell she was a classical sort of girl; everything in her house looked old-school.

"Your house is... very homey. The sculptures are cool." I placed my hands in my jacket pockets.

Jessica walks toward me with a bitter sexiness behind it. "The jacket's nice on you." She commented and fixed its collar. Her face was a little closer to me, her dress slightly brushed my leg, and her scent was like vanilla ice cream in the summer. She pulled away and retook my hand, leading me to the kitchen.

I was led to the kitchen to see one of the most amazing foods ever made. "The food smells amazing, Jessica," I said to her, amazed by how good it smelled and looked. I was a sucker for food, so this made my mouth water.

"Jess. Just Jess." She said as she smiled. "Please sit; this is my favorite dish for special guests." I sat down and eyed her intently as she brought a pan of something with white creamy sauce. The heat reached out to me and caressed what little facial hair I had. "Penna Pasta?" I raised my brows. She placed a plate in front of me and stopped in her tracks, "You know pasta?"

"I'm alright." I shrugged.

She nodded her head slightly. "Okay, I have a food connoisseur in my home." She then dipped her finger in the sauce and placed it in her mouth. She pulled her finger slowly and slurped the cream off. "I made the perfect sauce; please be my guest." She motioned to eat.

I chuckled, "Don't mind if I do." The evening pressed forward, and after two plates of amazing pasta and two glasses of wine, I was surprised I enjoyed myself. Jessica could indeed talk, but she made it all about me. I don't usually speak about myself, but she made speaking about my relationship with my parents comfortable. But my guts are never wrong; there had to be something off.

"Do you believe in love at first sight?" She asked. It was very random of her to ask me that, but I didn't think anything of it.

"It depends on the situation and the two people. In my opinion, love at first sight does not always work.

She didn't expect my answer by the look on her face. She just stared at me with a blank expression. She smiled randomly and shook her head slightly as if in a trance. "Ever since I saw you, I couldn't stop thinking about you today." She stated. "I just fell in love with you at first glance."

"Thanks... um, Jess. I'm flattered, really, but we just met?" I replied.

" I know, but didn't you feel our connection?" She asked me. I thought it strange when she began to declare her affection for me. I cut her off in the middle of her sentence, "Jess. I'm going to stop you right there. I appreciate your hospitality, but I think you misunderstood exactly what this is..." I swear my throat was drier than a desert.

She stared at me again as if I had said something terrible to her. It was only two minutes when she stood in the same position starting. "But... I love you, Darius Green. I made you my special pasta. I wore my favorite dress." She finally speaks as she trembles. Tears filled her eyes after her comment.

I didn't mean to offend her or make her sad. Don't get me wrong, she's fucking attractive, sexy as hell. But right now, I just met her. And I'm just a new guy in the neighborhood. "You're wonderful and kind and beautiful. But I'm just trying to settle in right now. I think if we get to know each other more as friends. Then maybe there can be something."

Her demeanor altered when I said that, not in disappointment but in anger. She remained silent after my remark and lowered her head for a few moments. When I asked whether she was okay, she threw everything off the table onto the floor. She yelled, repeatedly smacking herself. She stood there motionless, eyes locked on mine, and the tears streamed down her cheeks. That's when she fell on her knees, head down, and wept. Confusion was what I felt at that moment, and even then, when I felt sorry for her, I knew I had to leave that place. I got up and made for my house and never looked back. It would be a few days since my last encounter with Jessica Lewis; I wish the narrative could finish here—but it doesn't.

—

It was a long day of unpacking all the essential boxes and making the house feel complete. I was tired, but my mind was alive. I decided to watch some TV. My eyes began to be tired. Midnight came so fast. I felt like I was watching for just an hour. I got up and prepared for bed. The warm shower was rewarding after a long day of settling. That would be the night

I'd hoped to finally get complete rest since I'd been at the house. Nothing would compare to my first night's sleep. I could not get the picture of Jessica screaming, breaking the plates, and the look in her eyes. I shook my head as I put on my T-shirt, and that's when a loud bang came from the living room. I may have left the TV on. BANG! The thud was louder, more angrier. My breathing quickened, and I grabbed the snow globe my mother gave me for Christmas, a sign of her protection. I told myself in my head that this was stupid. At the same time, I had to do whatever I could to protect my home.

I walked into the living room; there was nobody there. The TV is off. Maybe it was all in my head? The room was bare, aside from the boxes I'd yet to unpack. But —one of my windows was smashed, and every single glass on the panel had fallen to the floor. "Dear God," I thought. It was completely shattered. I scanned the area, and there it was a giant rock. I looked next door, and all the lights were off. I noticed a large rock on the right side of the living room (someone had thrown it through the window). I couldn't call the cops since I did not know who did it. My initial reaction was to look out the window to see if whoever did this was still out there, but no one was in sight. A sharp pain shot through the top of my head—It knocked me out, and everything went dark.

—

A ringing resounded in my head, and I jolted, waking up. Where was I? This was not my house anymore. I tried getting up but quickly noticed all the rope tied all over me. "Help! Somebody! Please!" I cried and wriggled myself out of the rope, but it was no use. I groaned and bowed my head. My thoughts were: I'm fucking dead. Then someone giggled. "You're awake!" said someone. The voice surprised me; it sounded somewhat familiar but unlike anything I'd ever heard. "I'm relieved you're awake, Dar. I thought I murdered you for a split second, but I'm glad I didn't." It was Jessica as she walked out from a shadowed corner. Jessica's hair was messy, her eyes worn out like she hadn't slept in days. She was clutching a bloody rock in her hand, which was most likely the rock she hit me with.

" Jessica? What the hell are you doing? Why am I tied up?" My throat tightened, and fear consumed me. Her hair looks as if it hasn't been touched for weeks. Her eyes were bloodshot red, and that bright smile had turned into a sinister grin. " Don't worry, everything will be okay, Dar. I did not intend to hurt you; I just wanted you to myself." Her comments scared the fuck out of me. I didn't know what to do but became more furious and fearful for my life.

"What the hell are you talking about? Let me go!" I shouted. My anger couldn't be held in any longer. But I think that was the worst time to let my anger go.

" No! I can't let you go! You have no idea how much I love you. I've been fantasizing about us ever since I saw you." She drew closer to me, her eyes wilder, and grabbed my collar.

"When you rejected me...It just made me love you even more."

" What are you saying right now? I barely know you."

"Yet, our chemistry has risen above all." I wanted to yell—but I was too terrified to say anything. Right now, I know she's insane due to the fact a tiny thing would set her off and most likely kill me. I just sat there and listened to her ramble about her feelings for me.

"I'll show you that we're made for each other," Jessica added. " If necessary, I will use this rock again." She walks away, leaving me behind, still tied. I looked around for anything that could help me escape — everything in the room was dark so that I couldn't see anything. I tried once again but could not free myself from the ropes. I gave up because I was exhausted and dehydrated. I knew I wasn't going anywhere for a while—until an idea came to me, a risky one, but it saved my life.

—

Several hours had passed. My body had become sore from sitting, and the rope tightly wrapped around me.

The door creaked open, and the heaviness in my chest returned. There she was, in a silky red dress and maroon lipstick. Her black heels clicked loudly as she approached me. "Do you like it, honey?" She asked.

"What's the occasion?" I tried to be polite in my response.

"The occasion is you silly." She rubs her hands from her torso to her waist, feeling herself. "All of this—is all for you."

"I feel so special..."

" You should; I'm not doing this for no one. So you're a fortunate boy." Jessica approaches me, sitting on my lap as she pushes her body against me. She softly holds my neck, her eyes locked with mine as she bites her lips. " I'm going insane just looking at you. I want you..." She gently kisses me on the lips, neck, and cheek. "I know that you want me, mister. Your eyes tell you no, but your body tells you otherwise. She grabs my crotch—The way she looked and felt upon me gave me a feeling of erection. "Please let me go—I promise I won't tell anyone if you let me go."

"No, I want to have some fun." She said to me as she continued to kiss me.

" Take a look at me. We'll have a great time if you let me go." I lean in and kiss her on the neck. She shuts her eyes—and begins to clutch at me as I continue to kiss her around the neck. I begged her to let me go so that "I could do a lot more," and what I didn't expect was to feel her arms wrap around me, untying the rope around my hands. "Anything for you, baby..." She muttered in my ear, whispering.

I was free—my arms wrapped around her waist as I continued to kiss her. Both exchanged lips, and my hands gradually rose from her waist to her face. I grabbed her face as gently as possible. I squeezed both my thumbs hard into her eyes. Her shriek pierced my eardrums, but I dug deeper; the squishing sound intensified as blood began dripping from her eyes. I shoved her away from me and frantically started swinging, unable to see me. I exited the chair, slammed her to the floor, and ran.

I ran to the door, trying to open it as hard as possible. Fuck, it was locked, but it was something that was on the door that was making it more challenging for me to open. I said fuck it and ran upstairs. I was in the hallway, breathing as heavily as possible. I jerked around to see which room to hide in; so many fucking rooms in this house. I chose the one in the middle and quickly shut the door. I was in a bright white bathroom with light peach curtains and aesthetic decorations. I went further back from the door. I instantly grabbed my phone to call the police. I told them what was going on as they were listening. The caller told me police officers were on their way and would be here in 10 to 15 minutes. That was too fucking long. What am I going to do for that long time?

I heard someone rushing up the stairs viciously. I knew it was Jessica. The stomps from her high heels were as loud as they could be. I tried to be quiet, putting my hand on my mouth to stop myself from breathing so heavily. The footsteps kept getting close as she came to a stop. Now, it was nothing but silence. I stood so still, not moving a muscle. I closed my eyes, shedding a bit of tears. Suddenly, something hit through the bathroom door, breaking off a piece. It was an axe that Jessica was carrying. She jammed the axe out from the door and hit it again, and again, and again. I jumped back inside of the bathtub, screaming. The more complex the axe hits the door, the louder it feels. She had broken a hole in the door, so big that I could see her.

Jessica entered the front door with a loud thud, breaking off the entire thing. My eyes widened as she held a giant axe, and blood was streaming down from her eyes. "You ungrateful piece of shit!" She yelled angrily as she approached me. "If I can't fucking have you—nobody will. You'll die like the others." She charged at me at full force and swiped down the axe.

I dogged but not fast enough, and she sliced my leg. I yelled and collapsed on the ground. I tried crawling, and her cackles echoed around the room as I did. Jessica jumps on top of me, choking me with the axe's stick. I use all of my strength to turn my body to the left, causing her to trip and crash into the wall. I get up, but the pain in my leg stops me.

I am pushed away from Jessica as she tries to draw me back to her—she is struggling. I took the axe in front of me, turned around, and threw the axe to her head without hesitation. She comes to a halt as blood drips from her skull. I didn't know if she was looking at me, but a thud came as she dropped to the floor, and I heard her last breath leave her body. I remained where I was, staring in disbelief at her body. Finally, I heard sirens in the distance...

—

It's been three fucking years since all of that happened. I still live in the same house; it's my sanctuary now. I couldn't afford to move right away anyway. I got here when all of that shit went down. Maybe one day, I'll leave, but I think I'm good right now. I always look at the house next door, waiting to see if the lights will all turn on, but they don't. No one has lived there after it all. Jesicca was telling the truth, too; they found four remains of men who had been missing for years. It's good that there are talks to take down the house and turn it into a playground. But I would be lying if I said I'm okay now. I have major trauma with night terrors. I keep having dreams of her on top of me, touching me, telling me she loves me over and over again. But I have my mom's snow globe. It reminds me I'm safe. It reminds me I get to live. Therapy helps a lot, but I'm afraid that even if she's dead. She'll continue to haunt me.

# 3
# THEY'RE LISTENING

I'm not sure how to tell this story; being the person who mostly keeps things to themselves—this is (there you should say) me stepping out of my comfort zone. My name is Sarah Williams, and what I'm about to tell you is something you may not find believable, but this will be a moment I will never forget because of how terrifying it was.

Now, We all experienced scary moments in our lives; some of us may have experienced home invasions, car accidents, or even watched someone die in front of us. I'm 31 years old, and I never experienced anything like that before.

—

Ten years ago, I was living in California—and going to school at Loyola Marymount University studying in arts. It was my 2nd year there, and I was going to school with one of my close friends, Michael. Michael was studying Journalism, so we barely had any classes together; we only saw each other whenever we were heading to get something to eat. Michael and I have been friends since our first year of high school, and ever since high school, he has always been into the whole theory of aliens, Men in Black, and Area 51. Every day we were hanging out, he would always talk to me about these theories he saw on the internet or on YouTube or some theories he had come up with. At the time, I didn't care or believe in aliens; I always thought the whole Area 51 thing was bullshit, but the way Michael explained his theories, he was very passionate about it—a little too intense, I must say. It got to a point where this passion of his went too far.

One day, Michael told me he and a few friends were camping for the weekend. I didn't think much of it, so I told him to have fun and not get into trouble. The way I'm telling this story will make you believe I and Michael were "dating," but that's far from the truth. My relationship with Mike and I are very close—basically, we see each other as siblings. I was the only child growing up, so Michael was like the brother I never had. When the weekend ended and a few days passed, Michael returned from his camping trip with his friends. I was curious about how the trip went for him ( due to him not being the camping-in-the-woods type of guy ), but I noticed something was a bit off from Michael because—he was acting strange when I saw him at school. When I walked up to him and asked how the trip went, he didn't respond and completely curved my question. I knew something was wrong, and this wasn't like him, so I asked him if he was okay. " Yeah, yeah, I'm good; I'm just a little nervous about this test in my math class, you know." He replied anxiously, slightly laughed nervously, and quickly walked away. I was worried because it's not like him to act this way—especially not for a test. I felt like something happened that weekend when he went to the woods with his friends, and now, looking back, my suspicions were correct.

I went to Michael's friends and asked them what was happening to him and what happened that weekend. To my surprise, they all responded that everything went fine, but they did notice him acting a little strange one night during the camping trip. They told me Michael went to the woods to use the bathroom while sitting in front of the campfire on the first night. They said he was in the woods longer than expected and began to notice. Before they went to check up on him, he returned, but his whole demeanor changed—and he was like that the entire trip. In my head ( not wanting to believe anything horrible ), he probably saw an animal or something and was just too embarrassed to tell me, so I just brushed it off.

I would be so glad if this story ended right then and there, but It gets worse. When days flew by, Michaels's behavior started to worry me. One day, he didn't show up to school and wasn't returning any of my calls. This was not like him because—for one— he always showed up every day, wasn't the type of student to miss school, and two—whenever he didn't pick up the phone, he always called back. I went to his dorm area and asked his roommate if he was there. They said no and that he's been out all day. To help me not jump to conclusions, I thought he went back to his parents and visited. Three weeks passed, and he never showed up. What set me off was that his Instagram, Twitter, Snapchat, TikTok, and Number were all deactivated. I called his parents and asked if he was there and if everything was okay with him, but they said he never visited. I told them that all of his social media, including his number, were deactivated and he hadn't shown up on campus—they got worried and called the police, and they filed a missing person report. I was terrified and had been thinking about him for the past few days because I hoped he was okay and safe.

One night, I was at home studying for my finals ( Stressing out as usual ). I lived in an apartment

THEY'RE LISTENING   27

because the dorms were too expensive. The place was small but was manageable for me ( since it was only me living here). Even with studying, I still had Michael on my mind—I mean, who wouldn't have their close friend on their mind if they were allegedly " Missing "? My phone began to ring ( startled me a little), and I stopped what I was doing and looked over who was calling. It was an unknown number, and I've been getting a lot of scam calls recently. And at first, I wasn't going to answer them—but something told me to answer.

I answered the phone, hoping to be a scammer trying to sell me something or telling me my bank account was overcharged (I wished that was the case ), but surprisingly, it was Michael on the phone—and hearing his voice made my heart drop.

"Hello, Sarah?" Michael said, whispering. " Oh my god, Michael, where have you been? I've been worried sick..." Before I could finish my sentence, he quickly interrupted me.

" Look, Sarah—I can't talk long on this phone. They're...listening."

"What are you talking about? Who's listening? Michael, what's going on?"

" When I went camping with my friends that day, I found something in the woods. Everything I theorized

—everything I read—was true. I found lost files, Documents, and real videos of what Area 51 has been doing for all these years. These files and documents confirm an alien invasion."

" Wait, what!?"

" Then these four guys—dressed in suits came to my dorm; they threatened me, saying that if I didn't get rid of these files—They would come back and kill me, my family, and my friends. So...I panicked and ran away and went into hiding."

I didn't know how to respond to all this; it made me feel overwhelmed and scared. An alien invasion was something I didn't expect to be a real-life thing, possibly, but at the time, I didn't care. I was more worried for Michael and wanted him to come home. I asked him where he was, and I wanted to go and get him. With a quick but defensive response, he told me no and that it was too dangerous.

" I don't have much time," Michael said. " I want you to pack your things and leave town for a few days. I think by being on this call, they might be after you as well." I had no clue where I was supposed to go. If this is true, what Michael was saying is that I didn't want to leave my parents behind, but at the same time, I didn't want to bring them with me and put them in any danger.

Suddenly, I heard a banging noise coming from Michael's end. It sounded like someone banging on the door—trying to get in. " Fuck! They found me. How did they find me?" Michael said, scared. I kept asking him what was happening, but he didn't answer. It was getting real for me—to the point, I started to cry and yelled at Michael to tell me what was going on. The door in the background suddenly opened, and it sounded like someone kicked it in. Michael screamed —and the call abruptly ended. When the call ended, every single part of my body was frozen. I couldn't believe what I had just heard, and every thought in my mind began to wonder—making me feel light-headed. I had to sit down for a minute; every part of my body shook in terror. I didn't know who it was that got Michael. I immediately called the police and told them what happened.

When I called them, one of the operators answered and told me what the emergency was.

" My friend Michael Phillips has been missing for a month now. After all this time, he called me, and I think he's in trouble."

" Okay, do you know his location?"

" No, I don't. I tried to tell him to give me his location, but he didn't listen. I don't know what to do, and I'm scared that something bad is happening to him." I didn't want to tell them what was happening, like the alien invasion stuff, because of how ridiculous it sounded. After that, the conversation instantly changed—for the worse.

" Well, I'm afraid your friend is gone...Sarah." The woman on the phone said my name. Even with me in distress—I don't remember me telling them my name.

" Wait, how do you know the name? I never told my name."

" If you don't keep your mouth shut, you will be gone too..." The call went to static after that, causing my phone to shut off completely. The fear in my heart rose even more in disbelief at what had happened.

I ran out of my couch toward the front door to get help. I opened the door—Three tall men were standing in my doorway. My heart dropped; my eyes widened like never before. These men were dressed in black suits—wearing hats. Faces were pale, no eyebrows, no particular features—Just plain. They looked at me without emotion, walking into my apartment and closing the front door.

" Who the fuck are you guys? What did you do to my friend?" I asked them aggressively.

" Your friend is no longer with us. So won't you if you say anything about what happened." One of the men told me. " Forget that this day happened and move on with your life. Suppose you say anything of this to anyone. Everything you call life will end. It will be asham of your family dying because of your big mouth..."

All of them then left the apartment, leaving me in distress and unable to think. Ten years later, Michael was never seen again. To this day, I haven't told anyone about what happened due to the fear of the black-suited men going after me and my family or something much worse. Everything that Michael said to me about the aliens, the invasion, someone knew and wanted him to keep quiet about what he saw or found—to the point where they threatened him and killed him. I'm living in North Carolina now, and I'm telling you this story now because I found the confidence to say it and share it, not worrying about the consequences that come after it.

# Acknowledgments

In 2022, I two short stories I had written but never really had the chance to release them. Now, I thought, why would these great stories have to sit in the vault, and I could release them as a short collection? The Girl Next Door was already a book that had been published, but I took it off and rewrote it and changed the ending a bit. I should say I love this story even better now.

I know this collection was small, but first time for everything. This won't be the last time I will make a short story collection. Thank you all for reading this, and happy days to all of you.

## About the Author

Jalen Tellis is an African-American author. He is known for his books with complex storytelling.

Milton Keynes UK
Ingram Content Group UK Ltd.
UKHW010040150524
442628UK00019B/186